The Riddle of the Spinning
Sycamore Seed

Written & Illustrated
by Ken Bowser

Solving Mysteries Through
Science, Technology, Engineering, Art & Math

Fitchburg Public Library
5530 Lacy Road
Fitchburg, WI 53711

Egremont, Massachusetts

The Jesse Steam Mysteries are produced and published by:
Red Chair Press LLC   PO Box 333   South Egremont, MA 01258-0333
www.redchairpress.com

 FREE Educator Guide at www.redchairpress.com/free-resources

For My Grandson, Liam

Publisher's Cataloging-In-Publication Data
Names: Bowser, Ken, author, illustrator.
Title: The riddle of the spinning sycamore seed / written & illustrated by
   Ken Bowser.

Description: South Egremont, MA : Red Chair Press, [2020] | Series: A
   Jesse Steam mystery | "Solving Mysteries Through Science, Technology,
   Engineering, Art & Math." | Includes a makerspace activity for hands-on
   learning about aerodynamics. | Summary: "While playing in her tree
   house, Jesse is intrigued by a falling sycamore seed that slowly spins
   to the ground. But when she sees acorns falling fast directly down to
   the ground, she must solve the riddle while learning about propellers,
   windmills, and using technology to understand aerodynamics"--
   Provided by publisher.

Identifiers: ISBN 9781634409391 (library hardcover) | ISBN 9781634409407
   (paperback) | ISBN 9781634409414 (ebook)

Subjects: LCSH: Trees--Seeds--Juvenile fiction. | Aerodynamics--Juvenile
   fiction. | Propellers--Juvenile fiction. | CYAC: Trees--Seeds--Fiction.
   | Aerodynamics--Fiction. | LCGFT: Detective and mystery fiction.

Classification: LCC PZ7.B697 Ri 2020 (print) | LCC PZ7.B697 (ebook) | DDC
   [Fic]--dc23

LC record available at https://lccn.loc.gov/2019936018

Printed in the United States of America

0520 1P CGF20

Table of Contents

Cast of Characters

Jesse Steam

Amateur sleuth and all-around neat kid. Jesse loves riding her bike, solving mysteries, and most of all, Mr. Stubbs. Jesse is never without her messenger bag and the cool stuff it holds.

Mr. Stubbs

A cat with an attitude, he's the coolest tabby cat in Deanville. Stubbs was a stray cat who strayed right into Jesse's heart. Can you figure out how he got his name?

Professor Peach

A retired university professor. Professor Peach knows tons of cool stuff and is somewhat of a legend in Deanville. He has college degrees in Science, Technology, Engineering, Art and Math.

Emmett

Professor Peach's ever-present pet, white lab rat. He loves cheese balls, and wherever you find The Professor, you're sure to find Emmett— even though he might be difficult to spot!

Clark

Jesse's next-door neighbor and sometimes formidable adversary. Clark Johnson is always with his slippery, slimy, gross-looking pet frog, Lewis. Yuck.

Lewis

Clark Johnson's slippery, slimy, gross-looking, giant pet frog, who lives in Clark's front pocket and goes everywhere that Clark goes. Yuck, yuck, and more yuck.

Dorky Dougy

Clark Johnson's three-year-old, tag-along baby brother. Dougy is never without his stuffed alligator, a rubber knife, and something really goofy to say, like "eleventy-seven."

Liam LePoole

A black belt in karate, and also the captain of the Deanville Community Swimming Pool Cannonball Team. Liam's best friend is Chompy Dog, his stinky, gassy, and frenzied brown Puggle.

Chompy Dog

Liam LePoole's very best friend and constant companion. Chompy is Liam's stinky, gassy and frenzied, little brown Puggle goes everywhere that Liam goes.

Kimmy Kat Black

Holder of the Deanville Elementary School Long Jump Record, know-it-all, and self-proclaimed future member of Mensa. Kimmy Kat Black lives near the Spooky Tree.

The Town of Deanville

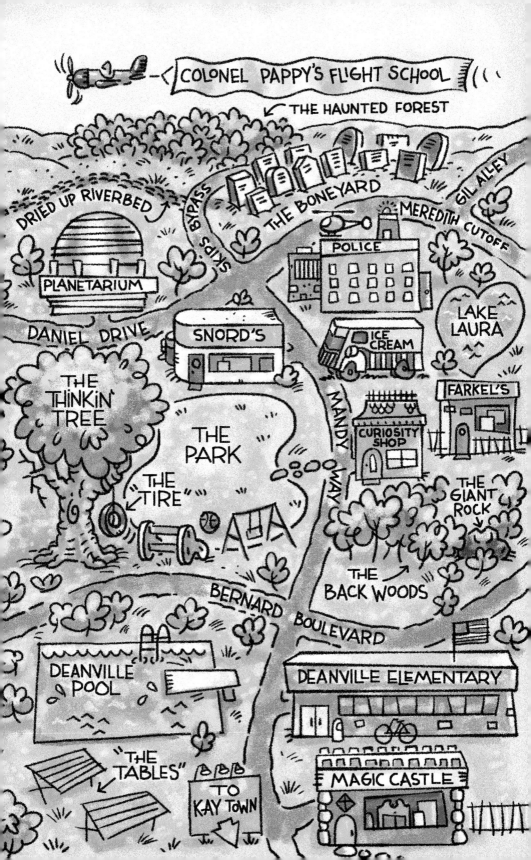

Spring Has Sprung. The Grass Has Riz. I Wonder Where My New Kite Is.

Chapter 1

"Do you know what I absolutely love about springtime, Mr. Stubbs?" Jesse Steam asked her snoozing cat, as she squinted up at the cloudless sky.

"It's not too windy and not too still. Not too hot and not too cool. It's just right." She smiled. "Take this breeze, for instance," she continued. "It's gentle enough to not mess up your hair, but just strong enough to keep these kites aloft," she said as she lay back in the afternoon sun.

Mr. Stubbs didn't seem to care. He was stretched out in the soft grass—toes up in the air as usual. He twitched his whiskers to shoo away the butterfly that was trying to land on his nose.

"I could lay here all day just watching these kites drift back and forth. Back and forth. Back and forth." Jesse yawned.

Just as Jesse spoke, a large acorn fell from the top of the big oak tree they were beneath and bopped Mr. Stubbs right on the top of his furry head. "Yowl!" Stubbs hissed as the nut bounced off of his noggin and on to the ground. As Stubbs regained his composure, a feather drifted down, ever so gently, and landed upon his pink nose. "You're a mess, Stubbs," Jesse joked.

The regular neighborhood gang was there. They had seen Jesse and Stubbs heading to the park with her homemade, diamond-shaped kite and decided that this was a great day for some aerial entertainment.

Kimmy Kat Black brought her beautiful, delta-shaped kite that was decorated in all of the colors of the rainbow. Liam LePoole had an interesting-looking box kite. "How does that crazy-looking thing even stay up in the air?" Jesse had asked him earlier in the day.

"Don't ask me." He laughed. "It just does!"

"It's a mystery to me, Liam," Jesse replied. "I guess it has something to do with the way the wind blows. I guess there's some scientific explanation, but I sure don't know what it is," she confessed. The kids marveled at just how gracefully the kites stayed up in the air in such a gentle breeze.

Jesse had spoken too soon when a huge gust of wind came out of nowhere, sending all three kites into a spinning frenzy. Liam LePoole's box kite spun around and around in the air like a pinwheel. Kimmy Kat Black's delta kite dived violently toward the ground, only to lift swiftly back up again high into the air, narrowly avoiding a brutal encounter with the earth.

"Whoa!" the kids all screamed as they tried to regain control of their uncontrollable flying contraptions. "This is crazy!" They all laughed.

Then suddenly—*SNAP!* The string on
Jesse's kite broke, and the only thing the kids
could do was sit and watch as it flew higher
and higher into the air. Over the trees. Over
the hills. Out of sight.

Everyone Knows It's Windy

Chapter 2

"Oh man!" Jesse lamented. "Well, that's a goner," she moaned as her homemade kite drifted entirely out of view. "I spent all day making that stupid thing."

As they caught the last glimpse of Jesse's kite, heading for who-knows-where, Liam's box kite came slamming to the ground with a thud and a loud crack. "Well, at least you still have yours," Jesse said.

"Yeah, I'm pretty sure I can fix it," he concluded.

Suddenly, Jesse heard a loud WOOSH as Kimmy Kat Black's delta kite came whisking right between her and Liam. "Watch out!" Kimmy yelled as the kite brushed by their heads. Then, as quickly as it flew by them, it bolted straight up and slammed right into the top of a tree with a blast of leaves and acorns.

"Well, I've had about as much of this fun as I can handle," Jesse said to Kimmy and Liam as they gathered up what was left of their kites.

"Me too," they both chimed in.

"I'm heading back home to see if I can piece this thing back together," Liam said as he lifted his mangled box kite.

"The only thing I can hope for," Kimmy sighed, "is for another good gust of wind to come along and blow mine down out of that tree." She grumbled.

Jesse looked down at Mr. Stubbs. "Okay, Stubby boy," Jesse said. "Let's skedaddle." She helped Mr. Stubbs into the basket on the front of her bicycle, and the gang pedaled away.

Rounding the corner at Lily Pond Lane near the Spooky Tree, the group rode up to the Duck Pond. They arrived just in time to watch Clark Johnson and his tag-along baby brother, Dorky Dougy, as they were about to launch a homemade sailboat on its maiden journey into Bruce Spring Creek. And who was at the helm? Clark's slimy frog, Lewis, of course.

"Lewis and Clark. Off on another wild rafting expedition." Jesse chortled to herself smartly under her breath.

The troupe took up by the banks of the Duck Pond and next to the little creek that fed it. Clark lowered the small, homemade boat and its slimy, green skipper gently into the stream. "I christen thee *S.S. Smelly Frog's Breath*," Clark announced with a snort. "Now shove off, sailor!" he commanded as he gave the tiny boat a firm push with his muddy shoe. Lewis let out a gulping croak.

Clark gripped the string attached to the stern. As the breeze filled the vessel's tiny sail, the boat began to waft its way down the stream and into the larger pond.

The eager spectators watched as the boat blew further from the bank. "Sure hope that sailor can swim!" Clark laughed out loud as the group watched anxiously.

Suddenly a gust of wind sent the tiny ship skimming across the pond. The slimy, green commander leapt from the helm and landed with a big, wet *SPLAT*, squarely on

top of Chompy Dog's head. "Hey, look! He's a herpetologist." Clark guffawed.

"Yeah. He's a herk-a-lof-ta-gust," Dougy said as Chompy sported the wet frog on his head.

"Not a word, Dougy!" They all laughed.

What Goes { Up Must } Come Down. Well, Kinda.

Chapter 3

Jesse had nearly forgotten about her wayward kite by the time the kids made their way down Byrd Street and up to her house. Just as the group reached her driveway, Jesse noticed a remarkable sight. Her kite, which at one time seemed long gone, was unbelievably lodged up in the sycamore tree that held Jesse's tree house.

"Well, I'll be a monkey's uncle." Jesse laughed to the group. "What are the odds of that? It actually found its own way home!" she continued.

"That's absolutely stupefying," Kimmy said as she looked with amazement at the kite.

"Yeah! Stoobi-fly-ing," Dorky Dougy returned.

"Not a word, Dougy!" The gang laughed again.

"Here, Stubbs," Jesse said to the cat in the basket. "Let me help you down while I climb up into the tree house." Mr. Stubbs had no intention of climbing up into that tree with the other kids. Not when there was a sunny spot in the grass to sleep on.

Jesse and the other kids scrambled, one by one, up the wooden ladder into Jesse's tree house. "Wow, this is cool up here, Jesse," Kimmy Kat Black said. "I can almost see my house from here," she marveled.

Jesse reached over the rail of the tree house and tugged on the kite's tail to pull it loose. With a few good yanks, the kite was free and floated ever so gently and slowly to the ground, right next to where Mr. Stubbs was sleeping. "Never thought I'd see that thing again," Jesse said, brushing off her hands. "It sure came down a lot slower than it went up." She chuckled.

Just as the kite landed softly on the

ground, a large sycamore seed spun slowly past the kids, twirling and whirling as it drifted away on the breeze on its way to the grass below.

The kids stood in awe as they watched the spinning seed glide through the air like a miniature helicopter. "I just love to watch those things," Jesse said with amazement. Picking up another seed from the floor of the tree house, they watched again as Jesse dropped it off the side. Like the one before it, the sycamore seed spun gracefully through the air, drifting all the while and landing in the soft green grass far from the base of the tree.

The kids gathered more of the light, delicate seeds and dropped them one at a time, just to watch them twirl to the earth below. Kimmy Kat Black dropped a large leaf, and it fell softly too, but did not spin or drift as far away as the seeds did. Clark dropped a large white feather that he found, and it fell just as gracefully as the other items. Now, it was Dougy's turn. He found a pine cone and dropped it over. Down it went, as straight as an arrow, and like the acorn before, it bounced off of Mr. Stubbs' head as it landed with a thud. "Well, that fell a lot faster than the other stuff!" The kids all laughed.

Gumballs, Rice Grains, Pennies & Popcorn

Chapter 4

Jesse yawned and stretched by her bedroom window the next morning.

"Hmm." She wondered as she noticed the sycamore seed that sat on her desk by the windowsill.

The sun shined through. She heard the chirp of a single bird perched outside on a branch.

"What made that seed spin as it fell to the ground?" she wondered to Stubbs. "Some of the other items like the leaf and the feather fell nearly as slowly, but why didn't they spin like the seed? And the pine cone?" She pondered. "It fell straight down like a rock. But why?"

Jesse reached for her messenger bag. It contained all of the things she used to help her solve daily mysteries. Her spyglass was there, along with her flashlight and journal. "Okay," she said to Mr. Stubbs, who was sleeping in the sunbeam on the corner of her desk. "Let's take a really close look at this and see what we can deduce." Jesse held the seed up with some tweezers and studied it very closely through the magnifying glass. She examined it from top to bottom. Front to back. Side to side.

After setting up her microscope, Jesse peered intently through the eyepiece at the sycamore seed. "Parts of this thing sure are thin," she mumbled to Stubbs. "Almost like paper. Maybe this has something to do with why it spins."

She sniffed it. She shined her flashlight through it. She bent it. She even tested its weight in her hand, but it was too light to feel anything. If she could only find some other item that weighed about the same for some further examination.

"I need to try something else," she said
to Stubbs. "This calls for my balance scale."
Jesse placed the scale on her desk and
dropped the sycamore seed in the small tray

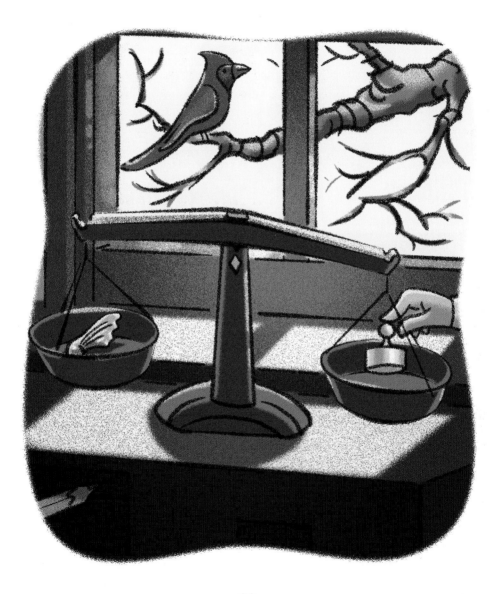

on one side of it. Then she took out her set of brass weights. "This is called a brass mass," she told Stubbs as she held one up. She placed the tiniest brass weight in the tray opposite the seed. "This is a one-gram weight," she said to Stubbs, who was watching intently. As she placed the weight in the tray, it quickly dropped to the desktop.

"Well, that's the smallest weight I have, Stubbs," she said. "So this seed weighs way less than one gram. I'll have to put several seeds on and do some math."

Jesse placed another sycamore seed on the tray, and then another, until the weight slowly lifted. "Well, it looks like three seeds weigh one gram, meaning one seed weighs one third of a gram," she explained to Stubbs.

"Now," she continued, "to find something of equal weight." She tried three marbles. Way too heavy. Next she tried three gumballs. Still too heavy.

Jesse thought and thought. "Hmm," she mumbled to herself. "What next?" She tried three grains of rice. "They're way too light," she determined. Then she tried three pennies. "Far too heavy." Finally, she tried three kernels of unpopped popcorn. "Well, that's right on the money," she said to Stubbs as the scale balanced out. "Three kernels of popcorn weigh one gram, which means one kernel of popcorn weighs about the same as one sycamore seed! Now on to some further testing!"

"OK, Stubby, old boy," Jesse said. "Now we have something that's basically the same weight as the sycamore seed. Let's make some observations," she said to the cat. Jesse stood up with the popcorn in one hand and the seed in the other. She dropped them at the same time and watched them fall to the floor. *Well?* she thought. "That's interesting, but I think we need a longer drop for a real

measurement," Jesse said. "Let's go to the tree house, Stubbs, my friend," she said to the cat. "That's the perfect place!"

Up in the tree house, Jesse held the popcorn and the seed over the rail, let them go together, and started her stopwatch. At first, they seemed to fall about the same. Then she noticed that the popcorn was falling straight down, while the seed twirled like a helicopter, drifting with the breeze as it fell.

The popcorn fell slowly, but when it finally landed in the soft grass, the seed was still spinning and floating on the wind. Jesse glanced at her stopwatch. "Four seconds," she said to Stubbs. "It took four seconds for the popcorn to hit the ground."

They watched as the seed continued to spin until it finally floated to a rest in the grass, far from where the popcorn landed. She clicked her watch to a stop.

"Twenty seconds?"

"I just don't get it." Jesse looked down at Stubbs. "The seed and the popcorn weigh the same. Why did the popcorn fall straight and land right below us, while the seed spun around and drifted further away? It stayed in the air five times as long." Jesse was mystified.

The Professor Professes To Profess

Chapter 5

"Are you asleep again already?" Jesse yelled down to Mr. Stubbs from the tree house. Stubbs was stretched out and snoozing in the sun beneath the tree.

She double-checked her stopwatch. "Yep. Twenty seconds." She made a note in her journal.

Jesse did the experiment three more times, with three more sets of seeds and popcorn, with the same results each time. The popcorn fell straight down, while the seeds spun and drifted away.

Just as Jesse was checking her stopwatch one last time and jotting down some final notes in her journal, she heard a recognizable voice from below.

"What in the world are you up to now, Jesse girl?" Professor Peach inquired from the sidewalk below. He was a retired university professor and lived next door.

"Hey, Professor," Jesse called back. "I'm trying to find out how and why in the world this sycamore seed falls so differently than everything else I test it against. I tested it against some popcorn that is the same weight as the sycamore seeds. But, while the popcorn falls quickly, straight down to the

ground, the sycamore seeds spin and twirl and take five times as long to land," she told the Professor.

"Ah ha!" he said. "Another mystery, eh? Well, you are the inquisitive one, now, aren't you, Jesse?" the Professor said warmly. "Climb down from there and let's have a look," he advised. "Maybe I can explain."

Jesse put the seeds, the popcorn, and all of her other stuff back in her messenger bag and climbed down from the tree house. Mr. Stubbs was waiting for her with Emmett, the Professor's pet white rat. Emmett was always with the Professor and eating cheese balls.

"Let's see what we have here," the Professor inquired. Jesse handed him the sycamore seeds.

"Ah," he said. "The seed of the *Platanus occidentalis*, commonly known as the American sycamore. Also called a maple tree," the Professor professed. He was always professing something.

"I can see why you're so perplexed," Professor Peach said as he studied the seeds carefully.

"Why, Jesse, my dear," he said. "This has nothing to do at all with the weight of your control items. This is a simple matter of aerodynamics and autorotation!" he surmised. The Professor loved to surmise.

"Aerodynamics and autorotation?" Jesse questioned.

"Yes. It's quite simple, my dear Jesse. Come by sometime and I'll explain it to you in great detail," the Professor offered.

Aerodynamics, Autorotation, Brain Racking & a Frisky Feline

Chapter 6

When Kimmy Kat Black poked her head into Jesse's kitchen window the next morning, she could tell that Jesse was deep in thought. "What's on your mind there, Jesse?" Kimmy asked.

"Oh, just thinking about these sycamore seeds again," Jesse replied, holding one up.

"Those old things?" Kimmy asked. "Man, you just don't let stuff go, do you?" Kimmy smirked.

"Not for a minute," Jesse replied. "I love a good mystery. I spent all day yesterday racking my brain trying to figure out why these crazy things spin to the ground while everything else just falls straight down," Jesse explained to Kimmy Kat Black.

"I even made sure that the things I was testing against were of the same weight,"

she complained. "Not only did the sycamore seeds drop slower and spin as they fell, but they also drifted far from where everything else landed."

"Ya got me, Jes," Kimmy Kat Black returned. "Seems to me that it *should* have something to do with how much they weigh."

"That's what I thought," Jesse said. "But Professor Peach came by and said it had something to do with aerodynamics and autorotation. Whatever the heck that is," Jesse continued.

"Ha ha!" Kimmy Kat Black laughed out loud. "That sounds just like something the Professor would say, doesn't it?" Kimmy giggled.

"You're right." Jesse smiled. "Yeah, he told me to stop by the next time I saw him out on his porch, and he would explain it all to me."

"Well, then I say we make a morning of it, Jes," Kimmy Kat suggested. "As a future member of Mensa, I feel it's my duty to educate myself about such matters," she bragged as she straightened her collar.

Jesse finished the few chores she had to do around the house, and Kimmy helped just to get them out of the way quickly. Stubbs the cat, however, was of no help whatsoever. Jesse tried three times to straighten out her bed, and each time Mr. Stubbs scrambled beneath the covers, only to mess them up again before poking his furry, orange face out from under the blankets. "It's a good thing you're adorable, Stubby boy!" She laughed as she scratched his fuzzy orange head.

The kids finished up at Jesse's house and marched over to see if the Professor was out on his porch. "Hey, Professor!" Jesse hollered as she saw him sitting out in his chair.

"Hey there, kids!" The Professor waved back.

47.

Flapping Things and Rotors and Wings

AERIOS
+
DYNAMIS
=

Chapter 7

On the short walk over to the Professor's house, Jesse and Kimmy ran into the usual gang—Clark, Liam, and Dorky Dougy.

"Pull up some chairs, kids," the Professor said. Jesse and the group gathered around the Professor's small table and listened intently.

"So you want a lesson in aerodynamics and autorotation, eh?" Professor Peach asked. "Let's see what we can learn," he lectured. "Let's begin with aerodynamics," he said as he began to write and draw on his large chalkboard.

"It's interesting to note," the Professor said, "that the word *aerodynamic* comes from two Greek words: *aerios*, concerning the air, and *dynamis*, which means force. So, simply put, 'aerodynamic' means *the force of the air,*" he proceeded. "Aerodynamics affects the motion of giant airplanes, tiny birds, a beach ball thrown near the shore, or a kite like Jesse's flying high overhead," the Professor explained.

"Anything that flies utilizes the principles of aerodynamics to move through the air. Airplanes and helicopters are designed and created by people, while birds—and other

LIFT

flying animals, such as insects and bats—owe their natural ability to fly to Mother Nature," Professor Peach asserted with authority.

"Airplanes are able to fly because of two effects. The first is the 'push' given by the plane's engines, which thrust the airplane through the air. The second effect is the movement of air over the airplane's wings, which creates the lifting force required to keep the airplane lifted up in the air. In simple terms, the wings of an airplane generate lift force, while the engine creates the thrust to propel the airplane through the air," he continued. "Lift is the same principle that causes your ball cap to fly off of the top of your head if you ride your bike very, very fast." The kids laughed.

"For birds, the flapping of their wings creates both lift *and* thrust. So if a plane could flap its huge wings, it wouldn't need engines," the Professor explained.

The Professor drew an interesting diagram on the chalkboard. "But it would be very difficult to build an airplane with giant flapping wings, wouldn't it?" Professor Peach snickered at his own silly joke.

"So the next time you toss a paper airplane, you'll know that there are aerodynamics at play, and the better the aerodynamic design of your paper airplane, the farther and straighter it will fly," he proposed.

"Now let's discuss *autorotation*," the Professor said. "Helicopters are another type of flying machine made by people. Like airplanes, helicopters also rely on aerodynamics to fly. However, they also rely on autorotation. Unlike an airplane, which flies by using wings that don't move, a helicopter flies using blades called rotors that rotate or spin around and around very fast. These 'spinning wings' cause the

helicopter to lift up off of the ground," the
Professor stated as he continued to draw on
the board.

"And just as you suspected, Jesse,"
Professor Peach went on, "the sycamore
seed is Mother Nature's version of a little
helicopter." The kids all laughed.

Windmills, Tubines, Parachutes and Mother Nature

Chapter 8

Professor Peach continued at the blackboard. "However," the Professor said, "Mother Nature uses autorotation differently than we do with man-made things, and for different reasons," he said. "We use helicopters as tools for transportation and to lift heavy objects," he explained. "The sycamore seed is designed by nature not to lift, but to fall to earth ever so slowly, and for long distances."

The Professor drew a large diagram of a sycamore seed on the blackboard. "Now, you'll notice if you look closely, kids, that the long, flat portion of the seed resembles the wing of a bird or an airplane. It also resembles the blade of a helicopter. In fact, these types of seeds are actually called *winged seeds* for that very reason," the Professor went on.

"These *winged* characteristics create *autorotation,* or automatic rotation that causes the seeds to spin, much like a helicopter blade. But instead of lifting the seeds up, it allows them to fall gently to the ground when it's time for the tree to drop its seeds. However, Mother Nature had something else up her sleeve when she designed the winged seed," he pointed out to the kids. "The design of these seeds also allows them to drift for long distances on the wind. This way the sycamore tree and others like it can cast their seeds far and wide, so that the tiny seedlings that spring up from them have plenty of room to spread their roots, limbs and wings," the Professor said proudly.

The kids marveled at the diagrams that the Professor drew and at how he explained aerodynamics and autorotation. "Wow!" the kids said together.

"Who knew that Mother Nature was so smart?" Kimmy Kat Black returned.

"Ah, my dear Kimmy." The Professor smiled. "You'd be amazed at the important lessons you can learn from observing Mother Nature."

The kids and the Professor spent the rest of the morning discussing aerodynamics and

OLD
WINDMILL

MODERN WIND
TURBINE

PINWHEEL

autorotation, and the many places they can be found in nature and in man-made tools.

"Take the common windmill, for instance," the Professor went on. "Windmills have been in use for thousands of years. They convert energy of the wind into rotational energy by the means of sails or blades. Windmills were used to turn stones to mill grain, pump water, or both. Modern windmills take the form of wind turbines, and they are used to generate electricity," he instructed. "So now let's have some fun and see what we can make using aerodynamics!"

While the kids watched, the Professor showed them how to make a simple pinwheel using a straw and some construction paper. "Now you have your own mini-windmill." The Professor laughed as he blew on it.

Then he showed them how to make a small parachute using a piece of a plastic

bag, some string, and a small weight.
"This parachute, kids," he went on, "also demonstrates the effects of aerodynamics. By catching the air, much like the seed did, the parachute falls ever so slowly to the ground."

With the Professor's help, each of the kids made their own pinwheel and parachute. They then spent the rest of the day holding the pinwheels in the breeze and watching the parachutes glide to the ground as they dropped them from Jesse's tree house.

"Aerodynamics sure is fun!" Clark was heard to say. "Yeah! Daro-maniacs is sure fun!" Dougy repeated. "Not a word, Dougy!" The kids all laughed.

THE END

Jesse's Word List

Adorable
something that's really cute—like you

Aerial
happening in the air—like a smelly toot

Aloft
up in the air—like your hand is when you really need to be excused from class to go the bathroom

Authority
someone who thinks they can boss you around

Chortle
to laugh—*He chortled as I stepped in dog poop.*

Contraption
a weird machine or device—like a toilet

Deduce
to find something out—*I deduced he was a dork when he chortled as I stepped in dog poop.*

Herpetologist
someone who studies gross, slimy reptiles

Inquisitive
curious—*I was inquisitive as to why he chortled.*

Jot
to write something quickly—*I jotted, 'I'm a dork' on a piece of paper and stuck it on his back.*

Lament
to express sadness—*I didn't lament about the note.*

Mangled
to destroy—*he mangled the note when he found it.*

Miniature
very small—*I thought the miniature note was small enough that he wouldn't notice it on his back.*

Mystify
to be bewildered—*I was mystified when he found it.*

Observation
to see something for yourself—*I made an observation that he was a dork.*

Ponder
to think about—*I pondered whether I should leave.*

Racking
to think really hard—*I racked my brain about what he'd do.*

Skedaddle
to leave quickly—*Heck, yeah, I skedaddled!*

Snicker
a suppressed laugh—*When I got home, I snickered so much that I almost peed my pants.*

Thrust
to push—*The next day he thrust the note in my face.*

About the Author & Illustrator

Ken Bowser is an illustrator and writer whose work has appeared in hundreds of books and countless periodicals. While he's been drawing for as long as he could hold a pencil, all of his work today is created digitally on a computer. He works out of his home studio in Central Florida with his wife Laura and a big, lazy, orange cat.

Try It Out!

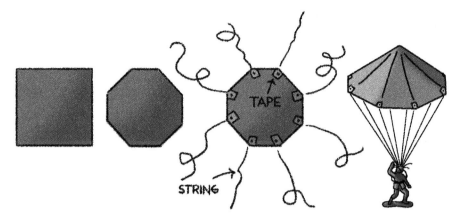

Make a Toy Parachute!

Parachutes are used to slow the motion of an object as it falls through the atmosphere. The word "parachute" comes from the French expressions for "protect against" and "fall". Parachutes protect pilots, soldiers, and skydivers from falling too fast and getting hurt.

What You Need: Lightweight plastic grocery bag, safety scissors, hole puncher, 8 pieces of string cut to the same length, clear tape, and a small toy

Steps:

1. Cut the grocery bag down to a large flat square. Trim off the corners so you now have an octagon (8-sided shape).

2. Use the hole punch to punch small holes near each corner. Put clear tape over the holes as reinforcement, and then punch holes again.

3. Tie one end of each piece of string to each hole. Pull the other ends of the 8 pieces of string together and tie them in a knot.

4. Push your small toy through the knot. Now you have a parachute! Hold the parachute out in front of you, above your head, and release it.